Samuel French Acting Edition

Tiny Houses

by Chelsea Marcantel

SAMUEL FRENCH

FOR PRODUCTION ENQUIRIES

UNITED STATES AND CANADA
info@concordtheatricals.com
1-866-979-0447

UNITED KINGDOM AND EUROPE
licensing@concordtheatricals.co.uk
020-7054-7200

be invented, including mechanical, electronic, photocopying, recording, videotaping, or otherwise, without the prior written permission of the publisher. No one shall upload this title(s), or part of this title(s), to any social media websites.

For all enquiries regarding motion picture, television, and other media rights, please contact Concord Theatricals Corp.

MUSIC USE NOTE

Licensees are solely responsible for obtaining formal written permission from copyright owners to use copyrighted music in the performance of this play and are strongly cautioned to do so. If no such permission is obtained by the licensee, then the licensee must use only original music that the licensee owns and controls. Licensees are solely responsible and liable for all music clearances and shall indemnify the copyright owners of the play(s) and their licensing agent, Concord Theatricals Corp., against any costs, expenses, losses and liabilities arising from the use of music by licensees. Please contact the appropriate music licensing authority in your territory for the rights to any incidental music.

IMPORTANT BILLING AND CREDIT REQUIREMENTS

If you have obtained performance rights to this title, please refer to your licensing agreement for important billing and credit requirements.

TINY HOUSES was received its world premiere co-production by Cincinatti Playhouse in the Park (Blake Robison, Artistic Director; Buzz Ward, Managing Director) and Cleveland Play House (Laura Kepley, Artistic Director; Kevin Moore, Managing Director) in Cleveland, Ohio on March 29, 2019 and in Cincinnati, Ohio, on May 4, 2019. The performance was directed by Laura Kepley, with sets by Arnulfo Maldonado, costumes by Amy Clark, lights and projections by Elizabeth Mak, and sound by Daniel Perelstein. The production stage manager was John Godbout. The cast was as follows:

CATH..Kate Eastman

BOHDI ....Peter Hargrave

JEVNE...Nandita Shenoy

JEREMIAH ....James Holloway

OLLIE ....Michael Doherty

TINY HOUSES was developed as part of Chautauqua Theater Company's New Play Workshop series in 2016, underwritten by the Roe Green Foundation. It was further developed as part of the New Ground Theatre Festival at Cleveland Play House in 2018, with the support of the Roe Green Award.

CHARACTERS

CATH – (20s-30s) Serious but funny, insecure, somewhat anxious. Relocated to Oregon from New York to build a Tiny House with Bohdi. Used to work in finance.

BOHDI – (20s-30s) Pron: BO-dee. Determined, self-satisfied, fanatical. Throws himself fully into a new pursuit every six months. Charismatic; in another life, he could lead a cult. Grew up in Oregon, and moved back from New York to build a Tiny House with Cath. Works as a life coach and productivity counselor. White.

JEVNE – (20s-30s) Pron: JEV-nee. Quiet, seemingly flighty, but with a strong core. Bohdi's childhood sweetheart, who still carries a torch for him; she's not a man-stealer, she is patient and believes she has prior claim. Works as an ASMRtist on YouTube.

JEREMIAH – (30s-40s) Plain-spoken Tiny House construction consultant hired to help Bohdi and Cath. A solid, sturdy kind of person who sees things clearly and speaks with conviction. He is a finisher.

OLLIE – (20s-30s) College friend of Bohdi's who is letting Bohdi and Cath build their Tiny House in his backyard. Enthusiastic, easygoing, guileless. He is a shepherd. Has a South African accent. Sells haunted dolls on eBay for a living. White.

Bohdi and Ollie are white men. The other parts may be played by an actor of any race. The cast should include at least one person of color.

SETTING

The suburbs of Portland, Oregon.

TIME

The present.

SCENES

Scene One	The Trailer (Week 0)
Scene Two	The Floor (Week 2)
Scene Three	The Wall Frames (Week 16)
Scene Four	The Roof (Week 24)
Scene Five	The Siding (Week 30)
Scene Six	The Windows and Doors (Week 34)
Scene Seven	The Tiny House (Week 36)

Perhaps the weeks are projected onto the stage at the top of each scene, to help the audience keep track of time.

THE WORLD

The play takes place in the backyard of Ollie's house, in a mid-sized town in northern Oregon, not far from Portland. If possible, it would be awesome if the walls and floor of the stage could be covered in very green grass (realistic or fake-looking).

The action spans nine months.

Over the course of the play, a Tiny House is built onstage. This can be built from any materials that fit the budget of the theatre: it can be foam core and cardboard, or paper, or anything that suits. The important thing is that a physical house takes shape, and that it takes physical effort to build it. People should be constantly working on the house in Scenes Two to Six; characters rarely leave the stage once they are introduced. There may be times that additional work is required in the transition between scenes to get the house to where it needs to be in its construction. If this is the case, we should see and hear it all, underscored by sound design.

There is much opportunity for storytelling in the transitions. Who is building what, with whom, when, and in what spirit gives the audience a lot of information with which to supplement the text. Please choreograph and design accordingly.

Scene One
The Trailer (Week 0)

(Lights up on the backyard. There is a small frame trailer sitting there, the kind you would attach to the back of a truck, with nothing on it. Downstage there is a microphone on a stand. **JEVNE** *enters and speaks into the microphone. She is recording an ASMR video, and her voice is soft and soothing; she is trying to relax us.)*

(Note: The ASMR video portions of the play should not actually put people to sleep. **JEVNE** *should not whisper.)*

JEVNE. Good evening. It's so nice to see you again. I decided to make a simple, relaxing video for you this time, using my new microphone. You can tell me your opinion of it in the comments below. I'm going to include some of the most requested triggers as of the last few weeks, and I hope this video will give you tingles, and help you drift off into peaceful dreams. So put on your headphones, close your eyes if you want to, and just relax.

> *(***JEVNE*** *takes a small makeup brush out of her pocket and begins gently brushing the microphone. It makes a soothing sound.* **CATH** *and* **BOHDI** *enter and start walking around the trailer, inspecting it. They are playful and loving throughout the scene. They do not acknowledge* **JEVNE**, *and she does not acknowledge them.)*

One of the most requested things recently has been ear brushing. So I'll do that now, if you'll allow me.

(She brushes.)

Your ears are so nice. They are a beautiful shape. And so clean. You have a great energy. Thank you for letting me brush your ears.

> *(JEVNE brushes the microphone a little more.*
> *CATH and BOHDI look at each other.)*

CATH. Okay, question for you. Is it too late to think about not doing this?

BOHDI. *(Amused.)* Oh come on.

> *(CATH climbs on to the trailer. JEVNE stops*
> *brushing and starts whispering words into*
> *the microphone.)*

JEVNE. Love, love, love, love.

CATH. I'm just looking at it now. Now that it's here. And I'm thinking...

> *(BOHDI pulls CATH to him and kisses her on*
> *the cheek.)*

JEVNE. Kiss, kiss, kiss, kiss.

CATH. *(Spreading her arms.)* This is it.

BOHDI. That's exactly the point.

> *(JEVNE begins gently tapping the brush or*
> *the microphone with her fingernails. It's a*
> *pleasant sound.)*

JEVNE. Home, home, home, home.

CATH. Just two hundred square feet. This is all I have to deal with.

BOHDI. The world gets bigger when you're living small.

JEVNE. Sleep, sleep, sleep, sleep. Goodnight my friends.

> *(JEVNE exits.)*

CATH. *(Reminding herself.)* Tiny is happy.

BOHDI. Tiny is happy. Exactly. A thirty-year mortgage is not the only path to self-actualization. This is our moment. We're doing this on our own terms.

CATH. Well, I think the trailer looks great.

> *(She bounces on it a little.)*

BOHDI. So great. Sturdy.

CATH. It's really happening. Our big adventure.

BOHDI. Our best idea. No turning back now.

> *(They are quiet for a short, satisfied moment.)*

Since the trailer's been leveled and the anchors are welded on, first thing on the docket is the foundation frame and the sub floor. We're also going to need to put in a vapor barrier before we do much else.

CATH. *(Indulging him.)* Say it again.

BOHDI. *(Playing along.)* "Vapor barrier."

CATH. You're the expert. I promise to live in it, if you actually get it built.

BOHDI. Oh, I'll get it built. I've read all the blogs and watched all the videos. My blueprints are bulletproof. It's ten percent how-to and ninety percent why-not. I figure it should take about three months, start to finish.

CATH. Uh-huh.

BOHDI. And I only need a few thousand dollars to get it started.

CATH. In addition to the three thousand dollar trailer I just paid for.

BOHDI. Babe, we've been over and over this. You finance the house, and I'll build it. When I get the money together, I'll buy the land. We agreed on this before we moved out here. If you're having cold feet about the Tiny House, don't blame it on money.

CATH. Okay, but realistically, we have finite resources.

BOHDI. *(Undeterred.)* The thing about money is, in the city, no matter how much you get, you always need more. But here, with this life, we could have enough. We could build it, and suddenly, then, we'd be living in enough. Isn't that why you're here? Don't you see this trailer this for what it really is?

CATH. I just...honestly? I didn't think we were going to get this far with it.

BOHDI. Sure you did! This was mostly your idea.

CATH. Uh, this was definitely *your* idea.

BOHDI. But I could never have actually done it without you! Don't you remember, the first time I brought it up, after –

<table>
<tr><td>BOHDI.</td><td>CATH.</td></tr>
<tr><td>your bamboo died.</td><td>my bamboo died.</td></tr>
</table>

CATH. Who kills lucky bamboo?

BOHDI. Your apartment in Murray Hill – that place was literally stifling. No natural light, no space, everyone on top of you and surrounding you on all sides. Screaming fights in the morning and loud music in the middle of the night. You couldn't keep a low-maintenance plant alive in there, much less a human being. And you said...

(He prompts her to finish the sentence.)

CATH. "I want to live in a place where I don't share walls with strangers."

BOHDI. Exactly. That was the germ of all of this. And here we are, three thousand miles from New York City, with peace, and quiet, and more natural light than we know what to do with. We're making it happen, babe.

CATH. *(She breathes deeply.)* You're right. You're so right.

BOHDI. Besides, what's a few thousand dollars to you?

CATH. It's not small change. I no longer have a job.

BOHDI. It sounds like a lot out of pocket, sure, but when all is said and done, we'll own a house for like $20,000! On our own land. You'll never have to live in another rental.

CATH. *(Conceding.)* I cannot live in another rental.

BOHDI. What's the point of working seventy hours a week to afford a huge apartment you never have time to enjoy?

CATH. No point.

BOHDI. We don't need to buy a bunch of stuff to feel good about ourselves. We don't need to consume in order to be complete. It's a perfect marriage of environmental and economic action. We saved each other from the road more traveled. We are making a statement.

CATH. And now we're going to live in that statement.

BOHDI. You'll get a job you really love in Portland, and I'll be able to help more people. We'll be able to travel, and spend lots of time with our friends and my family. Every day, we'll have the chance to be a new and better version of ourselves.

CATH. *(Short pause.)* The pictures just look so much bigger online than...this. It's like a bathroom.

BOHDI. But remember, it's not just about the four walls. We'll have our own land – a garden, and maybe a pond. We'll build a little freestanding deck and eat all our meals outside in the sunshine. In absolute peace.

> *(He hugs her.)*

This is going to be perfect. Our point of orientation in the universe.

CATH. That does sound nice.

BOHDI. Simple and serene. For the two of us.

CATH. I'm a little worried about that, you know. It's only ever going to be big enough for the two of us.

BOHDI. *(Pause. He lets her go.)* One thing at a time, Cath.

> *(**OLLIE** enters.)*

OLLIE. Wheels!

BOHDI. What?

OLLIE. It has wheels, man!

BOHDI. I know.

OLLIE. I thought you were building a house.

BOHDI. We are. But we have to move it out of your backyard eventually.

OLLIE. Nah, not really.

BOHDI. That's the whole point.

CATH. After Bohdi buys a piece of land for us.

OLLIE. But. (*He deflates a little.*) Okay.

CATH. But what?

OLLIE. I kind of liked the idea of you two living in the backyard, I guess. I signed up for that. I thought.

CATH. That's really sweet of you, Ollie.

OLLIE. So you're just going to build it here, and then haul it out to your land piece by piece on the trailer?

BOHDI. No. The whole house fits on the trailer.

OLLIE. Come again?

BOHDI. Yes. Since it's on wheels, we don't have to worry about building codes. That's the beauty of a Tiny House.

OLLIE. That's not a house, brother. It's a cell.

BOHDI. Didn't you look at any of the websites I sent you?

OLLIE. I've been really busy with work.

BOHDI. You work from home.

OLLIE. So that means I have tons of free time to look at blogs about baby houses?

CATH & BOHDI. Tiny Houses.

OLLIE. You're judging my job.

BOHDI. You're judging my house.

OLLIE. I am not! I'm just surprised.

BOHDI. The Tiny House movement is a legitimate expression of values.

OLLIE. And so is selling haunted dolls online.

BOHDI. No one's arguing with that!

OLLIE. You're not?

BOHDI. How could I?

(*A short, awkward silence.*)

CATH. Bohdi thinks construction will take about three months.

OLLIE. Only three months?

BOHDI. Maybe four, if the weather's really uncooperative.

OLLIE. To build a whole house?

BOHDI. According to the blogs.

OLLIE. But you don't have any construction experience.

BOHDI. I'll learn as I go. You can learn to do anything on YouTube.

CATH. And we can hire a construction consultant if we need to. There are lots of them in Portland.

BOHDI. We won't need to.

CATH. We could work it into the budget. We don't *have* to have, for instance, the reclaimed hardwood cabinetry.

BOHDI. Won't be an issue. I've got everything I need.

OLLIE. Let me know if I can help.

BOHDI. The point is to build it myself.

OLLIE. I'm just offering. My daytimes tend to be pretty quiet.

CATH. Yeah?

OLLIE. Most people buy haunted dolls at night.

BOHDI.	**CATH.**
Sure.	That makes sense.

OLLIE. *(Pause.)* How is the plumbing situation going to work? On your piece of land?

BOHDI. Well, we won't have running water, or at least we can't count on it, so we're planning to haul water in.

OLLIE. And just...poop in the woods?

BOHDI. No. No, Ollie. Composting toilet.

OLLIE. Won't that smell?

BOHDI. Read the blogs I sent you! All these questions have been answered.

OLLIE. That sounds like a real commitment.

BOHDI. It's the next stage of human evolution. "Do not trouble yourself too much to get new things. Things do not change, we change. Sell your clothes and keep your thoughts. I went to the woods so I could live deliberately."

CATH. Do not start with Thoreau.

OLLIE. Is Thoreau a thing?

CATH. For Tiny House people? Thoreau is a god.

BOHDI. Live deliberately. Less stuff. Solar power. Composting toilet. Tiny is happy.

CATH. *(Pause.)* How much is the solar panel going to cost?

BOHDI. We'll cross that bridge when we get there.

> *(They all look at each other.)*

OLLIE. Twelve weeks, you say?

> *(Lights dim on the backyard. **BOHDI** works through the transition. **CATH** exits.)*

Scene Two
The Floor (Week 2)

*(Lights up on the backyard. Most of a floor has been installed during the transition. A compound miter saw and a stack of loose boards sit downstage. **BOHDI** is working; he has a hammer. **OLLIE** enters and approaches the microphone. He speaks into it.)*

OLLIE. It is possible to make things appear to happen because you are expecting so much. I have fallen into this trap myself. It is possible to convince yourself that something paranormal is happening, when really the events have a perfectly normal explanation. When I bought my first doll, I was so excited about all the things I thought were happening, but looking back on it now, I think most of them were in my head.

*(**CATH** enters and inspects the almost-finished floor. She and **OLLIE** do not acknowledge each other. **CATH** circles the saw and pile of wood.)*

When buying a doll, you want to look out for a few things. First: the age of the item. Vintage and antique dolls are more likely to be haunted. It's just a fact. Secondly, be wary of dolls that are priced very high. Sellers with truly haunted items will want to get rid of them as quickly as possible, and may even cover the shipping. Thirdly, and most convincingly, see if the item has been relisted. If so, the last owner probably couldn't handle it, and that is a good sign that you're not going to get a regular, normal, un-haunted doll. Or a doll whose spirit has gone dormant. Which unfortunately does happen. And it's nobody's fault.

CATH. *(To herself.)* He said he was going to have this done in a day. Dammit.

OLLIE. Now for the good part.

> (**BOHDI** *takes the board from* **CATH** *and begins to hammer it in place.*)

CATH. You said you were going to have this floor done in a day. It's been a week.

BOHDI. I'm still getting the hang of everything.

OLLIE. There is nothing you can really do to prepare yourself for owning a haunted doll. You probably think, "I can handle it. What's the worst that can happen?" But the first time you experience actual paranormal activity, it will shake you to your very core. Sometimes the activity will be localized within the doll itself. Sometimes energy will shift things around in your home environment. You may have bad dreams. You may feel you are never alone. Their eyes may follow you everywhere you go. (*Pause.*) Please consider your children before purchasing a haunted doll from me, or anyone.

CATH. We only have the sublet for three months. If everything takes seven times as long as planned, we're going to be homeless way before the Tiny House is ready.

OLLIE. Your friends may make fun of you. You must insist that everyone treat the doll, and you, with respect. People very likely won't understand.

> (**OLLIE** *exits.*)

CATH. Where did you get the compound miter saw?

BOHDI. I rented it. And very good, by the way.

CATH. I've been reading up on the ins and outs.

BOHDI. Have you had any big insights?

CATH. Well… I know we've been talking about a square-style footprint, but, we didn't really discuss A-frames, and I saw some –

BOHDI. (*Interrupting, a bit hurt.*) I've been working on our blueprints for weeks, and you suddenly want to trash them because you saw some photos of A-frames?

CATH. Kinda?

BOHDI. We agreed on a square style. We discussed it *at length.*

CATH. Yeah, but I wasn't…maybe I wasn't paying as close attention…as I should have been. But now I am! All I do when I'm waiting to walk into job interviews is read Tiny House blogs and listen to Tiny House podcasts.

BOHDI. Okay. Why?

CATH. I want to help with the construction.

BOHDI. That's not our agreement.

CATH. You need my help!

BOHDI. I really don't. I've got it.

CATH. You really don't.

BOHDI. Our agreement is that you put up the money for materials, and I supply the labor. That's what we decided, so it's fair.

CATH. I don't care about fair if it means we're out on the street.

BOHDI. How much do you know about construction?

CATH. About as much as you do.

BOHDI. You're supposed to be looking for a job.

CATH. I am looking. But there aren't, like, a ton of finance jobs in Northern Oregon.

BOHDI. Are you saying there's nothing?

CATH. There's not nothing. But I can job hunt a few days a week, and help you out here, too.

BOHDI. *(Kindly.)* What's really going on here, babe?

CATH. Really? I'm not sure that I want to work in finance anymore. Being burnt out on my job was a big part of the whole quitting-and-moving-across-the-country-with-my-boyfriend. Of-four-months. Thing.

> (**CATH** *moves toward the lumber pile, picks up a piece of wood, and tries to figure out where it fits on the trailer.*)

BOHDI. *(Watching her with the board.)* I'm not sure about this.

CATH. Well get sure about it. I'm helping you. I want to put some sweat equity into this home of ours. Without exception, all the people on those blogs discovered at some point that they couldn't build a house alone. I'm asking you to discover that now.

BOHDI. Fine. *(Pause.)* You're going to need a pencil.

(**OLLIE** *enters with* **JEVNE**.)

OLLIE. *(Happily.)* I found this girl in the front yard.

JEVNE. *(Shyly.)* Hi, Bohdi.

BOHDI. Jevne?

(**BOHDI** *walks over to* **JEVNE** *and hugs her. She is delighted.*)

Guys, this is Jevne! She grew up next door to me in Beaverton.

JEVNE. We went to prom together.

BOHDI. What are you doing here?

JEVNE. I asked your mom, and she gave me this address.

BOHDI. That's amazing! It's so great to see you.

(**CATH** *clears her throat.*)

Oh, Jevne, this is Ollie, my best friend from college. And my girlfriend Cath.

CATH. Nice to meet you.

JEVNE. Hi.

OLLIE. Mutual, I'm sure.

(*A short, weird pause.*)

JEVNE. So your mom said you're building a house?

BOHDI. A Tiny House.

CATH. Capital T, Capital H.

OLLIE. It's not just a house, it's a lifestyle. But there will be no pooping in the woods. That was a question I had.

JEVNE. I don't think I understand.

BOHDI. The whole house will fit on this trailer.

JEVNE. How?

BOHDI. A living area and a little kitchen downstairs, with a sleeping loft above the porch.

JEVNE. That's so small for a person!

CATH. Two people.

JEVNE. Oh, you're both –

CATH. Yep.

JEVNE. Well that's cool. Neato.

OLLIE. Who wants beers?

CATH. Great idea.

BOHDI. Cath, maybe you can help Ollie?

CATH. What? Why?

BOHDI. I'd just...like...to catch up with Jevne. For a little minute.

CATH. *(With raised eyebrows.)* Huh. A little minute.

*(***OLLIE*** and ***CATH*** exit.)*

JEVNE. I think you're going to pay for that later.

BOHDI. *(Suddenly agitated.)* What are you doing here?

JEVNE. I wanted to see you.

BOHDI. Do you really think that's a good idea?

JEVNE. You said you wanted to see me, too. In your messages.

BOHDI. I was just being nice.

JEVNE. Oh please.

(She takes out her phone and reads.)

Me: "I heard you're moving back to Oregon." You: "Yep, that's true." Me: "Can't wait to see you." You: "Cool."

(She puts down her phone and looks at him like this was the most obvious invitation in the world.)

BOHDI. Maybe I did want to see you. But in like, a general way. Not here, just out of the blue.

JEVNE. Are you ashamed of me?

BOHDI. Of course not. But how am I going to explain to Cath who you are?

JEVNE. I'm not that hard to explain. I'm the same as I've always been. You're the one who left and came back with a New York haircut and a New York girlfriend.

BOHDI. What's your end game?

JEVNE. *(A little hurt.)* My what?

BOHDI. How do you foresee this going? Best case scenario?

JEVNE. I just want to spend time with you.

BOHDI. And.

JEVNE. You were really important to me. If you're building a new life here, I want to be part of it.

BOHDI. And.

JEVNE. *(A weak joke to break the tension.)* I lost my virginity to you.

BOHDI. Irrelevant.

JEVNE. It's anything but irrelevant. We dated for ten years.

BOHDI. It's not really dating when you're eight...

JEVNE. *(Interrupting.)* I was your first kiss, I was your first love – anything you have with anyone else rests on a foundation that was laid by me.

BOHDI. We were kids.

JEVNE. Is your life so different that we can't be friends as adults, too? I just want to be part of your life, in a real way, not just a short visit at the holidays and a phone call every few birthdays. Is your new life really so fragile that you have to shut me out?

      *(***BOHDI*** looks at her, saying nothing.)*

I can help with the house.

BOHDI. You can?

JEVNE. Yeah. I know about wiring. And insulation.

BOHDI. You absolutely don't.

JEVNE. But I'm organized and a quick study. Plus, basically all I watch is HGTV. And serial killer documentaries.

BOHDI. Won't this get in the way of making your videos?

JEVNE. I'll find the time.

BOHDI. I'm in love with Cath. That's not going to change. What we had was special, but it was a long time ago… and… And you want to help me build a house? To live in with her?

JEVNE. I'll find the time.

(**OLLIE** *and* **CATH** *re-enter with beers.*)

BOHDI. Jevne's going to help with the Tiny House.

CATH. She is?

BOHDI. She's very organized, and a quick study.

JEVNE. I am. It's true.

OLLIE. That's so helpful!

JEVNE. I hope so.

OLLIE. Well this is great. The four of us, all helping.

JEVNE. What do you know about?

OLLIE. *(Handing her a beer.)* Morale.

JEVNE. Okay.

OLLIE. And this is my yard.

JEVNE. Neato. *(Short pause.)* You have a bruise on your face.

OLLIE. Yeah. I woke up with it. I don't know if that was one of my dolls, or the thing that follows me from house to house.

JEVNE. *(Short pause.)* Do you miss Ireland?

OLLIE. Never been.

CATH. *(To* **BOHDI.***)* Can I talk to you for a *little minute*, Bohdi?

(**BOHDI** *follows* **CATH** *off to the side.* **OLLIE** *and* **JEVNE** *start poking around at the woodpile, then working on the house.*)

What the actual fuck?

BOHDI. Don't overreact.

CATH. However I react is the exact amount I should react.

BOHDI. Well, I mean, that's your perspective –

CATH. *(Interrupting.)* Who is she? What does she want?

BOHDI. She's an old friend. She's like, my *oldest* friend.

CATH. She seems odd.

BOHDI. She's not odd. And she wants to help.

CATH. When I said I wanted to help, you acted like I was way out of line. Then this crazy-faced person shows up out of nowhere, and suddenly, there's room for everybody?

BOHDI. If I don't let her help, I'll get a call about it from my mom, and it'll be a whole thing. This is how small towns work. *(Pause.)* Most of the people I knew in Oregon have moved away. We don't have many friends here yet, and I don't think Jevne has a lot of friends, either.

CATH. There's probably a reason for that.

BOHDI. Can't you give her a chance? Please? For my sake?

> *(**CATH** looks at him for a moment and makes a discovery. She's not threatened by it; on the contrary, she thinks it's cute and kind of funny.)*

CATH. Oh my god. You dated her, didn't you?

BOHDI. *(Minimizing.)* Girl next door.

CATH. You dated her for *years*. Oh, Bohdi, that's really kind of hilarious.

BOHDI. *(Slightly hurt.)* Why?

CATH. Because she's a loony tune. You must've been such a huge dork!

BOHDI. The past is the past; it doesn't matter. I love you. This is our house. It can't be anything but our house. Okay? Understand?

> *(A beat.)*

CATH. Have you told her she's going to need a pencil?

BOHDI. She knows.

> *(Lights dim on the backyard. **CATH**, **OLLIE**, **BOHDI**, and **JEVNE** work on the house.)*

Scene Three
The Wall Frames (Week 16)

(Lights up on the backyard. The floor is finished, and most of the frame of the walls has gone up during the transition. The saw is still onstage, along with a bigger stack of wood, some buckets, and more construction detritus. **OLLIE, CATH, JEVNE,** *and* **BOHDI** *are working.)*

*(***BOHDI*** steps away from the house and approaches the microphone. He speaks into it. He is beginning a motivation session. He speaks in a clear, confident voice. Perhaps music* underscores his voice; there is some noticeable effect on the microphone.)*

*(***BOHDI****'s video speeches are motivational in tone, markedly faster and more commanding than those of* **JEVNE** *or* **OLLIE***.)*

BOHDI. Let's begin with some breathing. We're going to breathe like babies. Babies breathe from their bellies, very gently and effortlessly. So what I'd like you to do is bring your awareness to your abdomen; you can even put your hands there if you like. As you breathe in, pay easy attention to the expansion. As you surrender the exhale, pay easy attention to the contraction. That's right. You're doing great.

    *(***BOHDI*** breathes in and out for a few moments.)*

If your mind wanders off, that's perfectly normal. Just bring your attention easily back to the sound of my voice. Focus on the breathing. Imagine turning

---

* A license to produce *Tiny Houses* does not include a performance license for any third-party or copyrighted music. Licensees should create an original composition or use music in the public domain. For further information, please see Music Use Note on page 3.

on a light bulb at the core of your being. Bring your awareness to your true power center.

CATH. If the studs aren't perfectly square, we're going to have roof issues.

OLLIE. I'm wondering how you plan to get a mattress in here once the walls go up. Won't fit through the door. Might want to store it inside the house until you need it.

CATH. Store it where?

BOHDI. Now that you're so fully aware of being in your body, connect to the universal source. Bring that light, that pure universal consciousness, right back down through your crown chakra, and fill your body with it.

JEVNE. I don't trust these anchors.

CATH. You don't trust them?

BOHDI. You're connected. You're present. You have the pure universal consciousness flowing through you. You are making yourself infinite. *(Pregnant pause, then he brings it home.)* You no longer need to smoke cigarettes.

JEVNE. All the literature says that the frame needs to be securely anchored to the trailer. The anchors look wobbly to me.

    (**BOHDI** *exits.*)

CATH. Let's just worry about getting the studs up, squaring them, and bracing them, okay? We'll test the security of the anchors after we do the sheathing.

JEVNE. There will be too much weight after the sheathing's done. We won't be able to make any changes, no matter what we find.

    (**CATH** *pulls several sheets of paper from her pocket and rifles through them. She thrusts a page into **JEVNE**'s face and stabs her finger at a line.)*

CATH. "*After* walls are raised, anchor plywood to foundation."

*(**JEVNE** takes a few sheets of paper out of her own pocket. After a moment of searching, she shows a page to **CATH** (much more tentatively).)*

JEVNE. "Frame walls and ensure squareness. Secure framing via anchors, *before* sheathing with plywood."

CATH. Why do *you* have printouts?

*(**BOHDI** enters with more construction materials.)*

*(To **BOHDI**.)* She printed stuff out.

BOHDI. What stuff?

JEVNE. A checklist.

BOHDI. *(Shrugging at **CATH**.)* Why is that a...?

CATH. Nevermind.

(A tense moment of silence. They work.)

JEVNE. Where were you this morning?

BOHDI. I had a new client! A smoker.

CATH. How did it go?

BOHDI. Well, it was her first-ever coaching session. But she wants to quit smoking really badly. So we'll see.

OLLIE. How many sessions does it normally take?

BOHDI. With some people, it's like a switch gets flipped in their brain the very first session, and they never have the urge again. With other people, it can take much longer. Some coaches don't even offer addiction counseling on principle.

JEVNE. Because it takes a while?

CATH. Because people lie.

BOHDI. Lots of times, people will say they want to stop doing something, but they're really just trying to get a partner or a parent or some other outside person off their back. And it's very frustrating when people aren't honest about what they want.

OLLIE. *(Joking.)* Or maybe you're just a crap hypnotist.

BOHDI. I'm a life coach and productivity counselor.

OLLIE. Whatever. I thought you wanted to be a pilot.

BOHDI. I thought you wanted to be an art auctioneer.

OLLIE. I thought you wanted to be a fitness model.

BOHDI. I thought you wanted to be a supportive friend! It's a real job.

CATH. Pffft. None of you have real jobs. That's why you live in Oregon.

BOHDI. *(Hurt.)* Hey! It takes a lot of balls to look a stranger in the face and say, "Follow me to your best life."

OLLIE. You don't have a job at all, lady.

CATH. But I have a résumé. And references.

OLLIE. I have an above-standard feedback rating.

JEVNE. I have five hundred thousand subscribers.

(They all turn around to face her.)

CATH. Half a million people watch your little videos?

JEVNE. My "little" ASMR videos are a recognized therapeutic technique! My voice can cure insomnia.

CATH. I don't think that's as great a thing as you think it is.

OLLIE. Yeah, I'd rephrase that. When you brag.

JEVNE. People send me donations and letters and gifts all the time, because they have tried medication and exercise and new bedding and new partners and new jobs and nothing has worked to soothe them but my videos. And Bohdi helps people to become their best selves. And Ollie…sells people haunted dolls. Which I guess they must probably want.

OLLIE. Oh, they want them.

JEVNE. *(A light, but barbed, attack.)* But all you do is take, Cath. You take people's money. It's cold. It's almost mechanical.

BOHDI. She's a little bit right, babe. *(To **JEVNE**.)* But Cath isn't sure she wants to do that kind of work anymore.

CATH. If I hadn't done that "mechanical" job, and been really good at it, for years, Bohdi, there wouldn't be any money to build this little house!

BOHDI. Tiny House.

CATH. All these two by twos and star drive screws and those anchors you don't trust, *Jevne*, were paid for by my cold, mechanical career. So you can shove your judgments right up your ass. I'm not from Oregon, so the idea of making money doesn't offend me. I'm perfectly happy to be the grown-up around here, if it means we can get some real shit accomplished within a reasonable timeframe. Does not bother me a bit.

OLLIE. *(Helpfully.)* Beers!!

(**OLLIE** *exits.*)

CATH. It is ten in the morning!

JEVNE. Don't be rude. Maybe that's when his culture starts drinking.

CATH. *(Pause.)* He's from New Zealand, right?

JEVNE. Well, I know he's not Irish. I thought it would be inappropriate to, like, ask.

CATH. It's not inappropriate to ask people where they're from. Wait, is it?

JEVNE. It feels inappropriate. It feels like, slightly xenophobic to point out that you noticed someone wasn't born in America.

CATH. Bodhi? Where's Ollie from?

BOHDI. I don't know. And we've been friends so long, it would be *really* rude of me to ask now.

JEVNE. Yeah.

CATH. Yeah, no. You're right.

(**OLLIE** *re-enters with beers. He passes them out. Work stops for a moment and they stare at the frame of the walls.*)

BOHDI. It's really coming along.

OLLIE. And only two months behind schedule. I'm impressed.

BOHDI. It's the rain. It rains all the time. I forgot.

CATH. Yeah.

JEVNE. Now I kind of want a Tiny House.

CATH. Of course you do.

OLLIE. Me too. Except I already have that big house.

(*He gestures to it.*)

It already exists. And it's bigger And I've buried a lot of stuff in the basement. So.

JEVNE. You could build a Tiny House for your dolls.

OLLIE. Nah. They'd destroy it. They have no respect for property.

JEVNE. Figures.

OLLIE. What can you do, really?

(*A short pause.*)

CATH. (*A new idea.*) What if we took out the window on the east wall?

BOHDI. The one above the sink?

CATH. No, the east wall.

BOHDI. The one above the chair?

CATH. Yeah. It would give us more storage.

BOHDI. More storage is the opposite of the point.

CATH. Right. Right.

BOHDI. We're not going to fill our Tiny House with a bunch of crap we don't need. We're going to prioritize authentic relationships. That's why we quit social media.

JEVNE. Oh *that's* why.

(*Everyone kind of looks at each other and sips their beers. They stare at the future house.*)

CATH. This is the "what did we get ourselves into?" point, isn't it?

BOHDI. Yes. When the walls go up, gravity starts fighting against you.

(*Sensing that the time is right for a motivational moment,* **BOHDI** *lifts his beer.*)

I'm so proud of this incredible team.

(They clink their beers together.)

CATH. It's taking forever, but we are definitely...doing this thing. And it's going to be amazing. I hope.

BOHDI. I, for one, am learning so much about myself through this process.

JEVNE. Me, too.

OLLIE. Me as well, I think!

*(They all look at **CATH** expectantly.)*

CATH. What? It's a house, not a miracle.

OLLIE. I mean. It could be both, right?

CATH. *(Shrugging.)* It has potential.

*(They gaze at the house. Maybe **JEVNE** crosses to put her hand on it.)*

JEVNE. I'm jealous of it. A little.

BOHDI. Of the Tiny House?

JEVNE. You're so sure that this will be home. I don't think there's any place like that for me. Not any building, anyway. My home is probably just wherever my parents are living. *(Pause, a realization.)* You can't really raise a family in a Tiny House, can you?

CATH. Oh, no, some people do. Lots of people do.

BOHDI. Most people don't.

CATH. Once we have the land, it would be a piece of cake to put on a permanent addition. Expand to five hundred square feet, or even a little more.

BOHDI. But that would defeat the point of having it built on wheels.

CATH. The point is to own a modest home and live a simple life.

BOHDI. But the point is also flexibility and freedom. Ergo, wheels.

CATH. Well, sure, but... *(Pause.)* People do raise families in them. It's not out of the question.

OLLIE. Of course not.

JEVNE. *(Short pause.)* I just don't see it.

> *(They put down their beers and get back to work. Perhaps something falls off the house or gets dropped. Crash! Lights dim on the backyard.)*

Scene Four
The Roof (Week 24)

*(Lights up on the backyard. The frames of the walls are finished, with spaces left for doors and windows. Rafters have gone up for the roof, and are partially covered with plywood. But something is off. Something is definitely not right with the construction; it looks wonky. The saw is still onstage, along with an even bigger stack of wood, and lots more construction detritus scattered around haphazardly, including empty beer bottles. The yard is a wreck. **OLLIE**, **CATH**, **JEVNE**, and **BOHDI** are working.)*

*(**CATH** steps away from the house, and approaches the microphone. She speaks into it. Perhaps she is on a job interview. Perhaps she is just trying to work through something for herself, the way she's seen everyone else work through things.)*

CATH. A hedge fund, you see, is very different from a bank or even a brokerage firm. A hedge fund is a specialized investment vehicle. It pools capital from a number of investors and finds the best bonds and securities and other instruments with which...to...

*(**CATH** runs out of steam. She starts over.)*

A hedge fund is administered by a professional firm, and it can be structured as a limited liability company, a limited partnership...or...

*(**CATH** is bored with herself. This identity doesn't fit anymore. She starts over.)*

Since we left the city I feel a little bit in exile from myself. I didn't know it was such a big part of my identity. I feel almost...embarrassed to live here. I ask myself all the time "where do you want to wake up?"

and mostly all of the time the answer is "not in the middle of the woods in Oregon."

Bohdi's been really evasive about having kids. I mean, we've only been dating for about ten months at this point, and it was all very exciting and romantic when I decided to quit my job and leave my friends and follow him out west into the wilderness, but this is kind of the dustpan of America, isn't it? Isn't that what they say? That the nuts and weirdos get swept as far west as they can, and when they can't go any further without falling into the ocean, they stick in Oregon? These people are weird people. They are not serious people.

> (**JEREMIAH** *enters, and looks at* **CATH. CATH** *turns to him and continues speaking into the microphone, but addresses her remarks to him now. No one else acknowledges him; they work.*)

I'm not saying I need to be around serious people all the time, I like fun, I'm a fun person, within reason, but I like to know that I'm always moving in an intentional direction. And I want kids. Not ten years from now. Soon. I was very clear about that with Bohdi, from the beginning. Ten months ago. And he seemed receptive to the idea, until we got here and started building. I thought we were coming here to build a home, so we could expand our life. But he's just interested in throwing everything away. Getting smaller. "Tiny is happy," and all that. *Babies* are tiny and happy!

I just don't know. There comes a point in any project where your excitement wears off, and there's still so much to do. Maybe relationships are like that, too. But it's so hard to ask for help. I've been so busy putting one foot in front of the other with this house, that I'm only now realizing that I might have made all the wrong choices. Maybe my gut is an idiot. Maybe I shouldn't be in charge of my own life, much less a child's. And what does Jevne actually want? And what is Ollie's deal? And does Bohdi love me the same way in Oregon that he did in New York? *(Pause.)* I stopped taking birth control. I haven't told Bohdi yet.

> *(A long pause.* **JEREMIAH** *and* **CATH** *stare at each other.)*

JEREMIAH. *(Slowly.)* I meant: "what's wrong *with the house*?"

CATH. *(Pause.)* Right.

> *(***BOHDI** *stops working and walks over.)*

BOHDI. Who's this?

CATH. I told you I was going to hire a construction consultant.

BOHDI. And I told you we don't need one.

CATH. This is Jeremiah.

JEREMIAH. Hi.

BOHDI. No.

CATH. What's wrong with you? Look at that roof! It's unhealthy. This isn't a tree fort. We have to live in it full-time.

JEREMIAH. Are you sure that's under thirteen and a half feet? You're not going to be able to transport it if it's even an inch over.

CATH. He's been playing fast and loose with the tape measure.

BOHDI. That's not true!

JEREMIAH. You said something about a skylight, Cath? Where's that supposed to go?

CATH. *(Pointing.)* Over the sleeping loft.

JEREMIAH. You didn't build headers for it? If you have to cut it out without headers, it's going to take twice as long. And I hope you installed collar ties if you plan to have a sleeping loft.

CATH. *(To* **BOHDI.***)* We didn't install collar ties. I don't think.

BOHDI. *(Under his breath.)* Shut up.

CATH. We need Jeremiah. A hell of a lot more than Jevne or Ollie. *(Loudly.)* No offense, guys.

OLLIE. *(Raising his beer.)* None taken!

JEVNE. *(Yelling from behind the house.)* I think I glued my hair to a truss!

BOHDI. Who's going to pay for him?

CATH. Oh, wait, is there an option besides me? Did you rob a bank?

BOHDI. *(Grudgingly.)* Fine.

(**BOHDI** *goes back to the house.*)

(Calling to her.) Jevne, do you need help?

JEVNE. *(Coming around the side of the house.)* Nah, just cut myself free again. Thanks.

JEREMIAH. *(To* **CATH.***)* Did you at least manage to leave the bottom edge of the window openings unsealed, for water drainage?

CATH. I think so?

JEREMIAH. What is the point of this?

CATH. The point of the Tiny House?

JEREMIAH. The point of spending a year building a structure that's not fit to live in?

CATH. It's not going to take us a year! It's only two hundred square feet.

JEREMIAH. It's going to take you a year. At this rate? No question.

CATH. Can't you speed things up? We're already over budget and we lost our sublet and had to move in with Ollie. *(Loudly.)* Which is so great!

OLLIE. Thank you!

CATH. But we can't impose on his generosity for an entire year. We've already turned his yard into Baghdad.

OLLIE. No worries! This is fun!

CATH. *(In a low voice.)* There are haunted dolls all over his house and I think they're giving me auditory hallucinations and nightmares. I need my own space.

JEREMIAH. Cath. Listen up. Speeding up construction for the sake of speed alone is going to cause you more problems than it solves. I can already see quite a few things I'm going to have to take apart and redo, and I haven't even really inspected the house yet.

Okay, it's a small structure, but it needs to be sound. It needs to keep out snow and rain and heat and not blow over in a windstorm.

CATH. Point being?

JEREMIAH. If you want to live in this thing for any length of time, and be happy, you need to stop being so anxious about how fast it's happening.

CATH. Oh my god. You're talking about my relationship.

JEREMIAH. I'm talking about your house.

CATH. Oh.

(*JEREMIAH starts to walk toward the house, then turns back to her.*)

JEREMIAH. I've helped a lot of couples build these Tiny Houses, and I do know one thing. Some people build them to keep stuff in, and some people build them to keep stuff out. And if you two haven't decided to build for the same reason, you're going to have a big mess on your hands before you're finished.

(*JEREMIAH goes over to where* **OLLIE**, **JEVNE**, *and* **BOHDI** *are working.*)

JEVNE. Hi. I'm Jevne.

JEREMIAH. What happened to your hair?

(*In lieu of a response,* **JEVNE** *hugs him.*)

OLLIE. I'm the aforementioned Ollie.

(*He motions toward the house with his beer.*)

So what does this look like to you?

JEREMIAH. (*Walking around the house.*) Well. The trusses are crooked, which is odd because the walls seem to be squared up. It's definitely too tall to fit under an overpass. House wrap looks okay. I think you need to do more alternating of one by twos, two by twos and two by threes to reduce the weight overall, while keeping it sturdy. I've already mentioned the problems with the sleeping loft and the skylight. We've got our work cut out for us, guys. We're definitely going to have to redo a fair bit. I'm going to need you to trust that I know what I'm talking about and follow my lead. *(Looking at* **BOHDI.***)* All of you.

JEVNE. *(Pause.)* I cut the window openings. *(Short pause.)* You'll probably want to remeasure the window openings. Put it on your list.

> *(Everyone is deflated.* **JEREMIAH** *sees how down they are.)*

JEREMIAH. This is not the worst case I've seen, guys.

CATH. It's not?

JEREMIAH. No. No. It's going to work. It's going to be a warm, attractive, extremely small house. And you'll both be very happy in it. But we have a lot to do. That's all. And no more drinking at 9 a.m.

> *(Everyone grumbles, ad-libbing.)*

Everybody needs to pull his or her own weight. Can we do that, team?

> *(Everyone is still a little skeptical.)*

CATH. Sure?

JEREMIAH. Come on. Convince me.

CATH. We can do it.

JEREMIAH. Still don't believe you.

CATH. We can DO IT!

BOHDI. Jesus, calm down, Cath. Of course we can do it. It's just not going to be very much fun.

> *(This is a shift for* **BOHDI.** *When things are no longer fun for him, the spark goes out of his passions.)*
>
> *(Everyone gets to work on the house. Lights dim on the backyard.)*

Scene Five
The Siding (Week 30)

(Lights up on the backyard. The wall frame looks perfect, and the roof is finished. The house looks great, no longer wonky. Half the walls are up. The saw is still onstage, along with an even bigger stack of wood, and lots more construction detritus. Large sheets of plywood lean against the structure, waiting to become walls. The yard is much more orderly than it was, but there is still a lot of stuff around. **OLLIE, CATH, JEVNE,** *and* **BOHDI** *are working.)*

*(***JEVNE** *steps away from the house, and approaches the microphone. She speaks into it. As she does, she taps the microphone gently with her fingernails; it is a pleasant sound. She speaks softly and soothingly.)*

JEVNE. Good evening, my friends. Thanks for joining me again. It's always nice to see you. I hope that you know how special you are to me, each and every one of you. I hope you know that I think about you all the time, and I want all good things for you, and I want you to be happy and healthy and safe.

OLLIE. Have you ever watched any of Jevne's videos?

BOHDI. I have. They're really relaxing.

OLLIE. Sometimes I put on headphones and listen to them as I fall asleep.

BOHDI. Me too.

CATH. You do what?

BOHDI. What? They help me fall asleep.

JEVNE. *(Taking a feather out of her pocket.)* Now that you're relaxed and calm, I would like to tickle you with this feather a little, but not too much. I hope this will help to soothe you even more.

> (**JEVNE** *begins stroking the microphone with*
> *the feather. It is, indeed, very soothing.*)

CATH. What are these videos like?

OLLIE. Lots of different things. Sometimes she reads things, like magazines or books or bedtime stories. Sometimes they're role plays, and she'll be like, a librarian, or she'll pretend to give you a facial.

BOHDI. I like the one where she pretends to give you a haircut.

OLLIE. Oh! That's a nice one.

JEVNE. I won't be playing any roles tonight.

CATH. Is it...sexy, or something?

OLLIE. No, that's not the point.

JEVNE. I don't have any special sound effects.

OLLIE. It kind of turns your brain to mush. You should check it out.

BOHDI. Sometimes she tells you about what's going in her life. Those are my favorite, actually.

CATH. But you know what's going in her life. You see her almost every day.

BOHDI. Right, but it's the tone of voice she uses. It gives me tingles. You just have to watch the videos, I can't explain it.

JEVNE. Tonight I want to give you a hopeful little message. To tell you a good story.

> (**JEVNE** *stops stroking the microphone with*
> *the feather. She holds it in her hand.*)

CATH. I guess I don't see the appeal.

JEVNE. Once upon a time there was a girl. She grew up next door to a beautiful boy. And they were both kind of odd, and they were both a little shy, but that was okay, because they understood each other. They could be their real true selves with each other, and that was fine. As they got a little older, the girl began to have sweet feelings for the boy. She grew her hair long, and changed the way she dressed, and wore perfume. The boy didn't notice.

> (**JEREMIAH** *enters. He's got a load of supplies in his arms.*)

JEREMIAH. I brought more furring strips.

CATH. Perfect. Can you help me tape the house wrap seams on this side?

JEREMIAH. Sure thing.

> (**JEREMIAH** *crosses to* **CATH** *and starts to help her.* **OLLIE***'s phone or watch alarm goes off. He looks at it.*)

OLLIE. Oh! Gotta go check on an auction. We might actually get Lucille out of the house, finally. If it's the right buyer.

CATH. Please. Oh, please god.

> (**OLLIE** *exits. Over the next few lines,* **BOHDI** *loses interest in what he's doing and drifts over toward the microphone and* **JEVNE***. Meanwhile,* **JEREMIAH** *and* **CATH** *are working closely. There is an obvious attraction between them.*)

JEVNE. (*Speeding up and coming out of her ASMR voice.*) He was all she thought about all day long. The sound of his voice turned her insides to hot chocolate. The mention of his name, even when he was nowhere around, made her blush. He was every good thing in the world, but she was sad. She knew that if she told the boy how she felt, and he didn't love her back, her heart would break into a million pieces.

CATH. I'm glad the rain let up, finally.

JEREMIAH. I don't mind the rain. It slows things down, sure, but otherwise I like it. Lived out in Arizona for a few years and I missed the rain.

CATH. Oh yeah?

JEREMIAH. Yeah, I have people out there. Thought it would be nice to make a change, live somewhere else, after growing up here. But I missed all the green. Not many plants in Arizona. And all the ones they do have are tryin' to kill you.

CATH. So you moved back to Oregon?

JEREMIAH. I did. Turns out they don't give medals for sticking with a bad idea, just to prove you didn't make a mistake. I'd moved just for the sake of moving.

CATH. Change can be invigorating. I've always thought.

JEREMIAH. Well, sure. But I already knew where home was.

CATH. You're… *(She searches for the word.)* rooted, Jeremiah. I admire that.

JEREMIAH. You aren't?

CATH. Oh no. I see every day as a chance to be a new and better version of myself.

JEREMIAH. What's so wrong with this version?

> *(A beat. **CATH** smiles. Something is happening here, between them.)*

> *(**BOHDI** is now standing near the microphone, looking at **JEVNE**. She continues to speak into the microphone, but now she's addressing her story to him. She strokes his face gently with the feather.)*

JEVNE. *(Speeding up and coming out of her ASMR voice even more.)* One day as they were walking home from school, the girl did the bravest thing she'd ever done in her short life. She grabbed his thin shoulders, pulled him toward her, and planted a big kiss right on his lips. And to her shock, and to her delight, the boy kissed her back. The boy loved her back. They loved each other for many years, and it was dazzling. *(Short pause.)* One day the boy left. He never said he would come back for the girl, but she knew in her heart that he would someday. They are meant for each other, and that kind of connection has no expiration date.

CATH. Did you sleep okay last night?

JEREMIAH. Not really. Insomnia's back. Ollie told me I should watch Jevne's videos to fall asleep.

CATH. And did you?

JEREMIAH. I did. I tried. I guess I don't see the appeal.

CATH. That's what I said!

JEREMIAH. She's just whispering at the camera. How is that a job?

CATH. Thank you.

JEREMIAH. Did Bohdi tape the seams on the other side?

CATH. *(Going around to check.)* He was supposed to. He didn't finish.

JEREMIAH. *(Joining her.)* Here we go. We'll finish it. *(Pause.)* Did you hang this siding?

CATH. Yeah. Got done last night after you left.

JEREMIAH. Looks great. You should be proud.

JEVNE. *(Now full voice and speed, no longer ASMR at all.)* The girl and the boy will always be connected. Nothing can change that, only delay it. They could each be married to a dozen other people, they could have a hundred babies with those dozen other people, and still, they would outlive them all. They will dig one hundred graves, waiting for the time to be together again. Which will come, it has to come, like sun follows rain. The girl is waiting for the boy to start the clock again.

> *(**JEVNE** and **BOHDI** look at each other. They almost kiss. They both want to kiss so, so badly.)*

CATH. This was all his idea, you know. And now I think he's losing the thread.

JEREMIAH. Then why are you still in it?

CATH. *(Pause.)* When I lived in New York, my life was like one-thing-next-thing-one-thing-next-thing-one-thing-next-thing all day long, every single day. And if I managed to, I don't know, make myself a sandwich and eat it, or stop and buy toilet paper on the way home from work even though I was exhausted, I would feel a moment of real accomplishment. A tiny moment of self-sufficiency, would be such a victory. And if I could do a little thing like that for Bohdi, it was even more satisfying. And I thought...what if I could have a life where all I did was things like that, real things? If everything I did, at the moment I did it, was the most important thing I could be doing? What if I weren't always working so hard to get to a next moment, somewhere in the future, when I could finally enjoy myself?

JEREMIAH. And have you found that life, here?

CATH. Nothing feels more important to me right now than building a place to live, and that's what I do all day. So maybe? Does that sound ridiculous?

JEREMIAH. Not at all.

CATH. I spent so many years being overwhelmed by the buildings I lived in. The garbage disposal would clog or the elevator would break or the doorknob would fall off and I'd have to call some other person to fix it and I'd feel so helpless. But you wouldn't feel that way, would you?

JEREMIAH. I couldn't fix an elevator.

CATH. But you could fix a doorknob.

JEREMIAH. *You* could fix a doorknob.

CATH. Now. I could now, yeah. I look at this building, and I can't believe I made most of it. It's an intimate space, I know every corner of it. It doesn't overwhelm me. *(Pause.)* I'm astounding myself. That's why I'm still here.

> *(A silence.* **CATH** *looks at* **JEREMIAH** *and* **BOHDI** *looks at* **JEVNE** *for a long moment. There is a sound and light cue, indicating a shift in time.* **CATH** *and* **BOHDI** *speak to each other, but they do not approach each other or look at each other.)*

BOHDI. Maybe I don't want to reinvent all at once. Maybe I just want to try to be a little different every day. Maybe I should focus on my shortcomings and fears, instead of always burying them in a project.

CATH. You were so excited in the beginning.

BOHDI. *(As he talks, he gets faster and more worked up.)* Maybe I'm not as worried about having stuff as I thought. Maybe it's okay to have lots of things that collect dust and make you anxious. Maybe money is more important than sleep. Maybe I'm not as concerned about off-gassing as I once imagined. Maybe I don't care whether or not the floors are reclaimed. Maybe I do want to eat food with growth hormones in it. Maybe I don't really know what parabens are so I'm not really scared of them. Maybe I can't live comfortably without high-speed internet. Maybe a Tiny House will turn me into a tiny person. Maybe the entire march of human progress up to this point – more, bigger, more, bigger, more – has not actually been wrong, but only natural, and we are not right to try to buck it.

> *(They face each other, and approach each other. They are both fighting hard to stay in a relationship that no longer suits either of them.)*

> *(***JEREMIAH*** works on the house, and **JEVNE** joins him.)*

CATH. You're overreacting.

BOHDI. The amount I'm reacting is the exact amount I should react.

CATH. We'll be finished so soon, and then we'll move in.

BOHDI. And...what?

CATH. Live.

BOHDI. But what will that be like? We have no space, we have no social life, we have nothing. You're not even looking for a job anymore. All we do is this, all day, every day it's not raining. And when we're not working

on it, we're planning it, we're measuring it, we're
fighting about it, we're pulling our hair out over it. We
could leave it. We could sell it.

CATH. No.

BOHDI. *(Pleading.)* This is all we are to each other now.

CATH. Is that true?

BOHDI. This is all we are to ourselves. *(Pause.)* What if it's
too easy?

CATH. A composting toilet is easy? Hauling in water is
easy?

BOHDI. What if it's too hard? *(Pause.)* What if you want
another big step, right away?

CATH. *(Quietly.)* Oh. *(She looks at the house.)* Are you saying
you don't want to build this Tiny House?

BOHDI. I do want to build it. I've always wanted to build it.
I don't know if I want to live in it.

> *(They stare at each other in silence. A spell is
> broken. Everyone can see and hear everyone
> else again.)*

What if I concentrate harder on finding our piece of
land? And you concentrate on finishing up the siding?
Just for right now. Just until I get my feet under me
again.

CATH. That's a good idea.

BOHDI. Yeah?

CATH. Yeah. A very good idea.

BOHDI. Great. I've saved some money. I should be able to
manage a down payment.

CATH. I didn't realize you were doing so well.

BOHDI. A lot of people around here are overeaters. And
alcoholics. It doesn't jive with the community aesthetic.
(Short pause.) Lots of people want to quit lots of things.

CATH. Great. Great for you.

> **(OLLIE** *enters, elated, even for him.)*

OLLIE. You'll all be happy to know Lucille has sold.

BOHDI. Which one's Lucille?

CATH. The doll that turns the TV on in the middle of the night and has no reflection.

JEVNE. Creepy.

CATH. I hate her.

OLLIE. That's why she's been acting up. She knows how you feel. I think she had some kind of abandonment trauma in her past life. She's very sensitive.

CATH. Just because I live with them doesn't mean I have to like them.

OLLIE. Yeah. But things would be a whole lot more harmonious if you did.

> (**BOHDI** *and* **CATH** *look at each other.* **BOHDI** *exits.*)

Where's he going?

CATH. I can't tell. It's happening so slowly.

JEREMIAH. *(Carrying a piece of siding.)* Little help with this?

> (**CATH** *goes to help him. They work. Lights dim on the backyard.* **JEVNE** *exits.*)

Scene Six
The Windows and Doors (Week 34)

(Lights up on the backyard. The house looks great. Windows are installed, but the door and skylight are not. There are spaces cut for these. The saw is still onstage, and the construction detritus mess has reached epic proportions. Ladders lean against the house. **JEREMIAH, OLLIE,** *and* **CATH** *are working. Perhaps one of them is on the roof.)*

*(***OLLIE*** steps away from the house, and approaches the microphone. He speaks into it.)*

OLLIE. It's important to remember that some vessels are very active from day one, and others take a while to get comfortable in their new homes. The spirits do not perform on command just because you want them to. You need to be patient, and allow the spirit and yourself to adjust. The worst thing you can do is get bored and put the doll in a corner and forget about it. You have not merely purchased a commodity, you know. You've agreed to provide a good home for a lost spirit.

JEREMIAH. You're going to be happy with that extra insulation this winter.

CATH. I think you're right. Especially since I won't want to run the propane heater at night. This place is essentially a tinderbox. Thanks for the advice on that.

JEREMIAH. That's what I'm here for.

CATH. That and the stimulating conversation?

JEREMIAH. Well, clearly. All of you are very easy to talk to. The only other person I ever discussed Arizona with is my therapist.

CATH. *(Impressed.)* You're in therapy?

JEREMIAH. It's *[current year]*, Cath. I handle my scandal.

*(On a different part of the stage, or perhaps at the back of the audience, **JEVNE** and **BOHDI** enter. They are far away from the others, checking out a prospective piece of land for the Tiny House. They look around.)*

OLLIE. I have a doll who was found bricked up in a wall with a mummified cat. I have a doll who was found at the bottom of an abandoned well. I have a doll who's already been sold a dozen times, and she's not even that old. I have a doll who likes to be kept in a case with lavender and acorns. I have a doll without a face that nobody wants. But I want him.

Everybody's got to have a home, don't you agree? It's business, sure, but it's also a good deed. To take in misunderstood dolls with limited prospects.

JEVNE. How many acres is it all together?

BOHDI. Two. Which I think is perfect.

JEVNE. Lots of room. You could put ten tiny houses out here.

BOHDI. Or one. Or a normal-sized house, with running water. And a chicken coop.

JEVNE. If you were the kind of person who wanted that. If you were the kind of person who valued the things he'd always known had made him happy. *(Pause.)* It's...

BOHDI. What?

JEVNE. It's a lot closer to town than I thought it would be. It's a lot more...on the grid, than I pictured.

BOHDI. Well, it needs to have access to county water and sewer and electric. For the chickens.

JEVNE. Chickens?

BOHDI. *(Very excited.)* I've been reading all about chicken farming. What you feed them can change the flavor, the nutrition, even the color of the eggs. Like, if you feed them a special diet with red peppers, the eggs are actually spicy. You can start cooking a meal, right on the farm! Chefs are going crazy for it. It's gonna be huge.

JEVNE. That's incredible! Does Cath know about the chicken plan?

BOHDI. No. Not yet. You're the first person I've told.

JEREMIAH. When we're done framing the door, we can test fit.

CATH. It's nice to have doors and windows. We'll be able to see in and get out.

JEREMIAH. Soon we'll be done building. You and Bohdi can move in, probably within the month.

CATH. He went to look at a piece of land today. With Jevne.

JEREMIAH. Are you excited?

CATH. I guess I don't really believe it will ever be done.

OLLIE. I have dolls that cause general, unspecified chaos. But I am determined to find them good homes. And if I can't? I don't have it in me to turn them out. Make sure to consider all of this before you commit.

JEREMIAH. Where is Ollie from, anyway?

CATH. Everyone's too sensitive to ask.

JEREMIAH. Hey! Ollie! Where are you from, man?

> (**OLLIE** *turns around, surprised and delighted. He steps away from the microphone and answers* **JEREMIAH.**)

OLLIE. South Africa. Thanks for asking!

CATH. Wow.

> (**OLLIE** *exits.*)

JEREMIAH. Easy.

CATH. *(Pause.)* I love Ollie. I love this yard. I hate those dolls. I might love Oregon? I definitely love this block.

JEREMIAH. Maybe Ollie'd let you stay here.

CATH. I don't think Bohdi would get on board with that. It's not Thoreau enough for him.

BOHDI. I think this is just the place.

JEVNE. Not a bad drive to your parents' place. Or my parents' place.

BOHDI. No it isn't.

JEVNE. Lots of room to expand.

BOHDI. Sure.

JEVNE. It's great, it's…has lots of…

> (**JEVNE** *is trying to say positive things, but all of a sudden, she stops talking. They stare at each other for a silent moment.*)

CATH. I can't believe it's almost finished. Because that means soon it will go back to being just me and Bohdi. In the middle of nowhere. In a house that I love so much more than he loves anything. And we won't see Ollie every day. And we'll have more and more fights and sex won't fix them. And I'll want him to want the things that I want, and he'll resist and resist until that resistance drowns us. *(Pause.)* And when this house is finished, you'll disappear.

JEVNE. *(Finally bursting.)* Pick me.

CATH. Don't disappear. You're the only person around here who doesn't have a stupid name.

JEVNE. Pick me.

CATH. You're the only person around here who is careful. Whose feet are firmly on the ground. Who isn't too polite to solve problems. I like you in my life, so much, and I'm terrified that all you know about me is this house.

JEVNE. Pick me over the house. Pick me over Cath. Pick me over New York. You don't need those things. I'm your true north, aren't I? I'm what drew you back here, I know it, even if you won't admit it. I've loved you my whole life. Pick me over some girl you just met. A banker? No one cares. You're supposed to end up with me. It's a better story. It means the world is a better place to live, if you end up with me.

CATH. I'm not just this house. I'm proud of this house, but I'm proud of other things. I'm proud of things I've discovered about myself, just in the last few months – some of the same qualities I admire in you, actually. *(Short pause.)* I love Bohdi, but I can't stand the thought of not seeing you every day. I know that's confusing. I hope that's okay.

JEREMIAH. *(Pause.)* You try new things. You take big leaps. I have to tell you, I'm comfortable with who I am. I think who I am now is who I'm always going to be.

CATH. That's okay. Not much wrong with this version.

BOHDI. A better story?

JEVNE. A better life. I'll make it so easy. You get big ideas and you want to chase them. I'll be your fixed spot. I'm strong enough. It's always been you, for me. I've tried to love other people, but I've never been able to mean it.

BOHDI. I have. I've loved other people, and I've meant it.

JEVNE. But it's not over. We're not dead yet. I will wait for you until I'm 100 years old, but I don't want to. Pick. Me. Now.

> *(Beat.)*

> *(**BOHDI** kisses **JEVNE**. **CATH** tries to take **JEREMIAH**'s hand, but he pulls it away.)*

JEREMIAH. Don't.

CATH. Don't?

JEREMIAH. I do know about you. Lots of things. I've been paying attention. And I like you, much more than I should. But you're with Bohdi. You're with him, and I hate that, but it's a fact. So I don't think we can be friends, really. It would make life harder for both of us. Do you see?

CATH. No. I don't.

JEVNE. *(Smiling.)* Neato.

> *(**OLLIE** enters. **JEVNE** and **BOHDI** exit, hand in hand.)*

OLLIE. Amazing work, guys! It'll be time to trim it all out soon.

JEREMIAH. Do you think you can handle that?

CATH. The trimming?

JEREMIAH. Between the two of you?

CATH. Me and Ollie?

OLLIE. Sure we can handle it. Everything okay, Jeremiah?

JEREMIAH. Something came up.

OLLIE. Oh no.

CATH. *(Pause.)* I can handle it.

JEREMIAH. I know you can. Best of luck.

(**JEREMIAH** *exits. There is a moment of silence.*)

OLLIE. I like that guy.

CATH. Me too.

OLLIE. I'm gonna miss him.

CATH. Me too. *(Pause.)* Bohdi's going to choose her, isn't he?

OLLIE. Choose her who?

CATH. Jevne. He's going to choose her, because she's uncomplicated and sure of herself and she'll never ask him to do anything scary. He's doing it now, isn't he? He's choosing her. My senses are all pricked up. I can tell it's happening. I guess it's been a long time coming.

OLLIE. I...don't know...the right thing to say.

CATH. *(Pause.)* I need you to help me put the mattress in the alcove. I'm going to use the sleeping loft for storage.

OLLIE. But...because –

CATH. *(Interrupting.)* Because a few months from now, it's going to be really hard for me to climb the ladder.

OLLIE. Oh! Cath! Congrat –

CATH. *(Interrupting.)* Stop.

(*A moment passes in silence.*)

OLLIE. So, um. What do you want to do?

CATH. *(Looking up.)* I want to put in the skylight.

OLLIE. No, I mean when... *(Pause.)* You can stay here, you know. You can leave the Tiny House parked here forever. You don't have to go.

CATH. I don't?

OLLIE. No. That's what I signed on for.

> *(**CATH** walks over and gives **OLLIE** big hug. He's ecstatic. It should be very clear that this is a totally platonic, brotherly hug, and not the start of a romantic relationship.)*

> *(**OLLIE** and **CATH** go back to working. Lights dim on the backyard.)*

Scene Seven
The Tiny House (Week 36)

(Lights up on the backyard. The house is totally finished; the door is closed. The saw and all construction detritus are gone. The yard is green and pristine. No one is onstage. The house looks so perfect and cozy and appealing.)

(There is a small solar panel set up beside the house, with a cord that runs to an exterior wall. There are Christmas lights around the front of the house, and perhaps a lamp inside it that we can see, but they are not illuminated.)

*(**BOHDI** enters and approaches the microphone. He speaks into it, confidently and clearly. This is a motivation session.)*

BOHDI. Take a deep breath in and hold it for a second. Now exhale. Another deep breath in and hold it... One... Two... Three... and exhale. That's good. Breathe into your head. One... Two... Three...

 *(**CATH** comes out of the house. We see her fiddling with the lights and the power cord. Something is not working.)*

You are a part of everything, and everything is a part of you. You are gaining command of the forces that control your life. You will be able to deal with anything that comes your way. Your new understanding of yourself will give you the power to make vital changes.

You will believe in your decisions. You will have the willpower to carry things through. You are making all the right choices. You are beginning to reconcile the world you want to believe in, with the world you do believe in.

(**BOHDI** *turns to face* **CATH**, *and steps away from the microphone. His voice interrupts her work with the lights.*)

Hi, Cath.

CATH. Hi, Bohdi.

BOHDI. *(Pause.)* The Tiny House looks great.

CATH. Thanks.

BOHDI. So, I guess you've wondered where I've been for the last two weeks.

CATH. Not really. I figured you were with Jevne. Then when Ollie told me he'd sent all your stuff to your mom's, I knew I was right.

BOHDI. Are you furious with me?

CATH. Of course I am.

BOHDI. You're hiding it really well.

CATH. It doesn't change anything.

BOHDI. It's not because I love her more than you.

CATH. Oh no?

BOHDI. No, it's just... This isn't supposed to be my life. I don't need to live off the grid. I don't need simplicity. I don't need to make things harder than they have to be. I don't need quiet. But I think you do, now.

CATH. Yeah. I do.

BOHDI. And I... I think you want...a family.

CATH. A baby. Yes. You know I do.

BOHDI. But I don't know that I do.

CATH. I told you from the beginning. I thought you were on board.

BOHDI. I get caught up in things. I got caught up in us.

CATH. We were a phase? Like Tiny Houses?

BOHDI. I guess. And a baby can't be a phase.

CATH. No fucking shit.

BOHDI. I... I just don't see the appeal. And I don't want to lead you on.

(*Beat.* **CATH** *makes the decision to keep her big news a secret.*)

Jevne can't do much on her own. She needs me. And you don't.

CATH. Jevne is not as helpless as you think.

BOHDI. You don't know her well.

CATH. She bagged *you*, didn't she? That was a neat trick.

BOHDI. It wasn't a trick. We are just...inevitable. (*Excited.*) We're going to raise chickens – gastronomically-enchanced eggs! It's the next stage of chicken evolution.

CATH. That's so great for you.

(*A moment of silence.*)

BOHDI. You'll find someone.

CATH. Stop talking.

BOHDI. And it's okay with me if you keep the Tiny House.

CATH. (*Surprised and angry.*) It's OKAY with you?

BOHDI. Yeah.

CATH. I don't remember ASKING you, if it's OKAY that I keep the house I paid for, and planned for, and finished after you abandoned it. And me! You needed me, for some reason, to get back here. Maybe it was just my money you needed, or my vote of confidence, I don't know. It doesn't matter. You took what you wanted from me, and I'm taking what I want from you. We're square. Run along.

BOHDI. You finished this by yourself?

CATH. Yes.

BOHDI. What about Jeremiah?

CATH. Haven't seen him in weeks.

BOHDI. And Ollie?

CATH. Ollie's been out of town since Monday. Something went wrong with Lucille's new home. He had to go sort it out with them in person. I guess Lucille was never going to have an easy transition. Truth be told, I a little bit miss that crazy haunted bitch.

BOHDI. If I'd known...

CATH. You don't have to know everything. It's not necessary or even advisable that you know everything. You gave up. I wasn't going call and cry and try to guilt you into helping me set up the solar panel and trim the windows. You checked out.

BOHDI. You're overly proud.

CATH. Oh no. You don't get to lecture me.

BOHDI. "I came to the woods so that I could live deliberately."

CATH. Thoreau's sister brought him lunch every day. You need to let Thoreau go. He was full of shit. Nobody does anything worthwhile alone.

BOHDI. *(Pause.)* This is the last time we're ever going to speak to each other, isn't it?

CATH. *(Deciding.)* Yeah. It is.

BOHDI. The house looks amazing.

CATH. Yeah. It does.

BOHDI. You're going to live in it alone?

CATH. I'm going to live in it with whoever comes next.

BOHDI. Here? In Ollie's yard?

CATH. For now. Ollie feels like home to me. I'm beginning to think it's people who are homes, not places. *(Short pause.)* I guess Jevne always knew that. I'm keeping Ollie.

BOHDI. *(Pause.)* It was a good experiment

CATH. It was a noble attempt. I admit that.

BOHDI. I'm gonna go.

CATH. I think you should.

> (**BOHDI** *turns to leave, then spins back around and hugs* **CATH**. *She lets him.* **BOHDI** *exits.* **CATH** *sighs.)*
>
> (**CATH** *is alone onstage. She goes around to the side of the house and fiddles with the solar panel. She plugs in the Christmas lights, but they don't work. She fiddles some more. No*

lights. She gets frustrated. She doesn't hear **JEREMIAH** *enter, and he doesn't say anything. He's a little dressed up, for* **JEREMIAH** *(like, he's wearing his nice jeans). After a moment, he startles her.)*

Dammit, Jeremiah! How long have you been standing there?

JEREMIAH. Not long. Two minutes.

CATH. What do you want?

JEREMIAH. You need help with that solar panel?

CATH. What do you want?

JEREMIAH. Should I have a look at it?

CATH. What do you want?

JEREMIAH. *(Fiddling with the panel.)* Everything looks right.

CATH. I can't get the electricity to come on. It's the final piece. I've been messing with it for two days. No luck.

JEREMIAH. Let me check inside.

*(***JEREMIAH*** goes into the house.)*

(From inside the house.) This is weird. It all looks right in here.

CATH. What do you want? Why are you here?

JEREMIAH. *(Emerging from the house.)* I never quit before. I don't skip over articles in magazines. I don't leave movies even if they're bad. It's the best thing about me. I'm thorough.

CATH. Well, you quit this. And now it's done.

JEREMIAH. I don't mean the house. I mean you.

CATH. That's ridiculous. You can't quit something you never started.

JEREMIAH. I let you down.

CATH. I didn't ask you to prop me up.

JEREMIAH. I promised to help with the house. I listened to your problems. And then I just dumped it all and left you to figure it out on your own. It's unprofessional. And unfriendly. I'm very good at finishing my commitments. Sometimes it can be hard for me to start new ones.

CATH. Look, I don't blame you. I put a lot of pressure on you that day, and I wasn't making much sense. I know that. I'm embarrassed about it now.

JEREMIAH. Don't be embarrassed.

CATH. I was involved with Bohdi, we were going to live in this house together, and you didn't want to disrupt that. I can't really blame you.

JEREMIAH. You <u>were</u> involved?

CATH. Yeah. Past tense.

JEREMIAH. Oh.

CATH. *(Lightly.)* Don't get any ideas. You're looking at my whole life, right here. My boyfriend ran off with a girl who puts people to sleep through the internet. I live in the backyard of a man who sells haunted dolls. I'm not qualified to do anything in Oregon, so I'll probably be getting a job at a coffee shop soon or a bar or a thrift store or a library. I hope. But you know what? I don't feel bad about any of it. I don't feel desperate. I'm pretty calm about the future. Because if I can build a house from nothing, I'm really not scared about whatever comes next.

> (**JEREMIAH** *and* **CATH** *stare at the house. The string of lights is still not on. The stage dims a little, as though the sun has set.)*

I just need some electricity.

JEREMIAH. I like this package.

CATH. Mine?

JEREMIAH. I like it. I'm not put off by any of that stuff.

CATH. No?

JEREMIAH. Nope. I came here, and I got to know you, and I admire you. I like you. You like me. I want to be with you, and now I can be.

CATH. That simple?

JEREMIAH. That's the way I see it.

> *(There is a pause. They look at the house.)*

CATH. *(Lightly, and very happily.)* In about seven months, I'm going to have a baby.

> *(**JEREMIAH** doesn't say anything, but turns to face the house, his back to the audience. **CATH** looks at the house as well. After a moment, **JEREMIAH** reaches over and takes **CATH**'s hand. At the same moment, the string lights around the house light up. A radio comes on inside the house, playing the perfect song (perhaps something like "La Vie en Rose"*). A tiny miracle.)*

> *(**OLLIE** enters, holding a doll that can only be Lucille. He takes in the house all lit up. He takes in **CATH** and **JEREMIAH** holding hands. He gasps.)*

OLLIE. Oh my god! Did you ever see anything more perfect in all your life?!

> *(They all stare at the Tiny House. The lights dim slowly.)*

> *(Blackout.)*

End of Play

---

* A license to produce *Tiny Houses* does not include a performance license for "La Vie en Rose." The publisher and author suggest that the licensee contact ASCAP or BMI to ascertain the music publisher and contact such music publisher to license or acquire permission for performance of the song. If a license or permission is unattainable for "La Vie en Rose," the licensee may not use the song in *Tiny Houses* but should create an original composition in a similar style or use a similar song in the public domain. For further information, please see Music Use Note on page 3.